This Book Belongs to

....

....

Published by Fledgling Press Ltd
1 Milton Road West,
Edinburgh
EH15 1LA

ISBN 9781912280216

Printed and bound by: MBM Print SCS Ltd, Glasgow

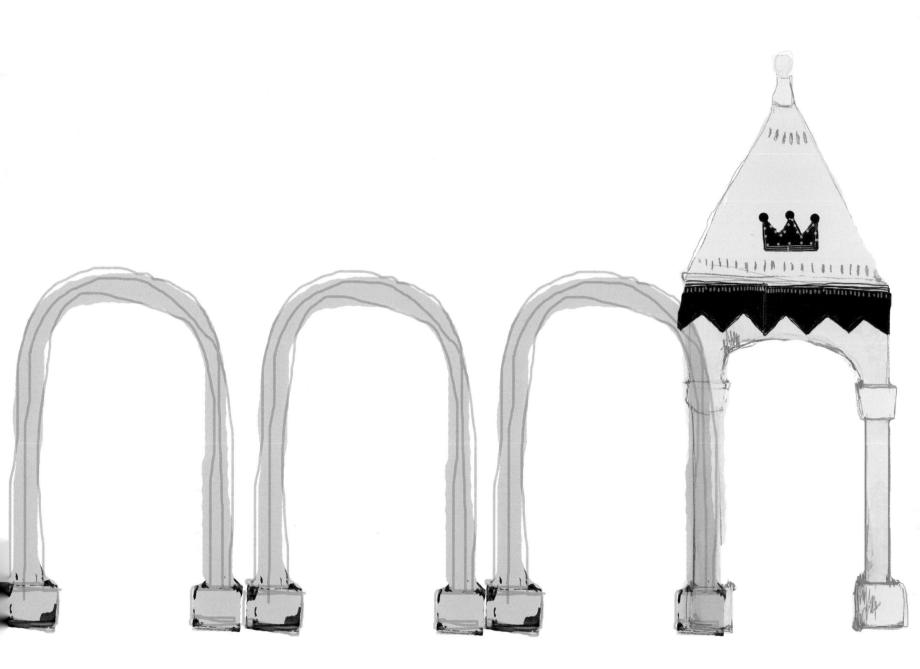

LEO AND THE LIGHTNING DRAGONS

WRITTEN BY GILL WHITE

ILLUSTRATED BY GILLI B

This book is for Leo.

Diagnosed with Ohtahara Syndrome, an extremely rare form of epilepsy, Leo suffers from a large number of seizures every day. Despite numerous treatments, these seizures remain uncontrolled.

Every day, my husband and I are amazed by Leo's sheer determination and refusal to give up and we could not be more proud of our boy, the bravest Knight we've ever seen.

All royalties from the sale of this book will go to

Children's Hospices Across Scotland

who have been a constant source of support to our family since
Leo was only a few months old.

With love
from Gill x

Mi b
x

LEO AND THE LIGHTNING DRAGONS

WRITTEN BY GILL WHITE AND ILLUSTRATED BY GILLI B

This is the story of **Leo**
The **BRAVEST** Knight of all

And what do Knights fight? **Dragons!**

That are **strong**

And **big**

And **tall**

But leo fought **different** dragons
They ATTACKED him from **inside**

And unlike all the other Knights

Leo had
NOWHERE TO HIDE

His dragons were not **big** nor tall
Blowing fire, but instead

They came disguised as **lightning** CRACKLING inside his head

They ATTACKED when he didn't expect it

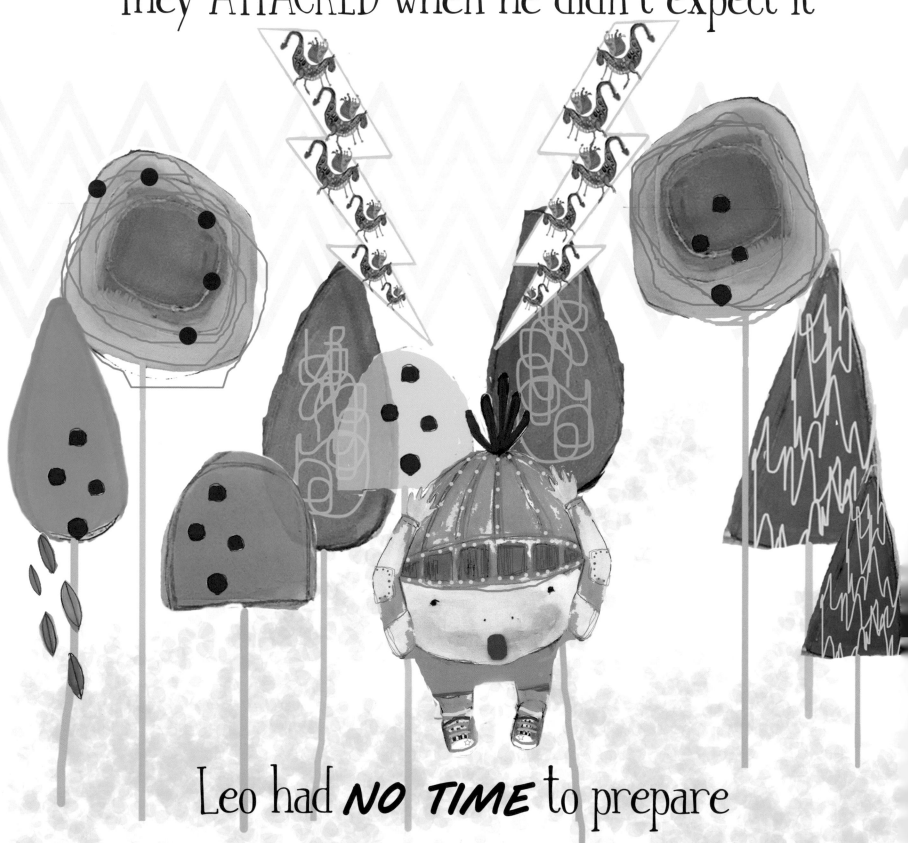

Leo had **NO TIME** to prepare

The people of the Kingdom were **angry**
And shouted " **This fight's not fair!** "

The witches tried to **help** him with **potions**
But the dragons were just **too strong**

The minstrels played music to **soothe** them
But they would not be **calmed** by a **song**

The wizard tried to POISON the dragons
By giving Leo MAGIC food

His mummy and daddy gave him *cuddles*
And did *everything* to *help* him they could

The people were **scared** for Leo

" He's not strong enough "

they said

"Those dragons **cannot** be defeated
But this made our hero see **red**"

" **Everyone** is trying to **help** me
And I'm **glad** I'm not ALONE "

"I'll show them **I CAN DO it**" he thought
"Then I'd really just like to go **home** "

The lightning CRACKLED and **exploded**
Inside our **BRAVE** Knight's head

But he **FOUGHT HARD**, as **HARD** as he could
Until the dragons turned and *fled*

Now Leo's fight is **over**
The dragons **forever gone**

He stayed **strong** and **didn't give up**
Until the battle was **won**

The townsfolk **gathered** and **voted**
They wanted Leo as their King

"You're the **BRAVEST** Knight we've ever seen"

They cheered "You can do anything!"

Leo ruled the Kingdom from that day
And lived his life **dragon free**

And the **proudest** of all of the townsfolk were **Leo's** **FAMILY**

It's fun to make a sensory story!

Here are some of our suggestions for bringing Leo and the Lightning Dragons to life.

Plasma balls are a wonderful way to show how the lightning dragons attack our brave knight.

Trying to find a 'HIDING PLACE' by draping material over the child's head and **whooshing** it away. Even hands over eyes would work!

Lots of items make **CRACKLING** noises. Our favourite way is to **shake** kitchen foil but you can use foil blankets, crinkly dog toys, salt shakers or rain makers.

You can see and hear the cauldron bubble simply by **blowing bubbles** in juice, water or milk through a straw! You can experiment with lots of different **smells** for the witches' potions, the **stinkier** the better!

Use slime, putty, dough, or even just a simple bowl and spoon to 'mix' your magic food.

See red by holding red tissue paper or red fabric over the child's eyes. Perhaps even pop on some red sunglasses or use red coloured fairy lights.

When dragons flee, they run and fly! Tapping your hands on a desk or on your legs for big dragon feet or waft paper or a fan for wide dragon wings!

Celebrate Leo becoming King by blowing trumpets! Use a kazoo or make your own with a comb and tissue paper!

And don't forget the cuddles!

Have some fun ideas of your own?

Visit us at www.leoandthelightningdragons.com and let us know!